Castle Capers

Written by Roger Befeler
Illustrated by Wil Foster

Across Treasure Bay and beyond the Emerald Mountains stands the mighty Great Adventures Castle. This ancient fortress is home to some valiant knights and their king. It's a magical place where almost anything can happen. One day, almost everything did.

It all started behind this drawbridge...

For weeks, King McBeard had been grumpy. He had never before been so grumpy for such a long time. The king noticed a small, gray cloud growing over his head. The grumpier he got, the bigger and darker the cloud became. His loyal knights and ladies could hear a faint clap of thunder when they passed the king.

One morning, rain dripped from the cloud onto the king's head. That *really* made King McBeard grumpy. Something had to be done. "Bring me the royal doctor!" ordered the king.

The royal doctor checked the king from his crown to his toes. "Sire," said the doctor, wiping raindrops from his stethoscope, "I'm afraid this cloud is the result of Cloudophobia, a rare illness that runs in your family."

He showed the king a scroll of the royal family. Sure enough, several ancestors had dark clouds over their heads. "The only known cure for Cloudophobia is to laugh a big, king-size belly laugh," the doctor added.

"I've been known to belly laugh," said the king hopefully. But try as he might, he could not even manage a small smile. "I challenge the royal court to make me laugh," proclaimed King McBeard.

Everyone showed off their funniest tricks.
Sir Gallant Hands juggled six helmets as he walked
on stilts, but the king was not amused. Lady Judy had
her puppets tell knock, knock jokes. The entire court
laughed—except the king. Finally, Jester balanced upside down
on one finger, a pig and a chicken wobbling on his upturned feet.
But not even this ridiculous sight tickled King McBeard's funny bone.

Meanwhile, high on a barren hill west of the castle, Eli the Wizard watched the goings-on at the castle in his crystal ball. The wizard had an idea he hoped might cure the king. Eli pulled out a book of magic from his shelf. Under "The Silly Spell" he read, "To conjure up a silly mess, say seven words that start with s. Point your fingers to and fro, and there some silliness will go!"

The wizard thought for a moment. "*Spaghetti, slobber, spider, stew, snarglewig, shabank, shaboo!*" he said. He pointed to the castle, and *zzap!* a giant lightning bolt lit up its craggy walls.

At the castle the next day, some amazing things began to happen. *Zzap!* the jousting knights and their horses switched places suddenly.

"Steady old boy!" said one horse to his knight.

"Neigh!" was all the knight could reply.

At noon, as was their custom, the knights tested the castle's cannons. As the cannonballs were fired, *zzap!* they became giant meatballs. This would have made quite a mess on the royal lawn, except that *zzap!* the grass turned into spaghetti. Then *zzap!* the water in the moat was spaghetti sauce.

Inside the castle, odd things happened, too. *Zzap!* the coat of arms grew arms, climbed down from the wall, and ran through the castle shaking hands with knights and ladies. The knights, whose armor was usually gold, *zzap!* found themselves wearing green polka dots or orange zigzags.

The king, sulking in his chamber, heard the commotion. "What's going on?" he asked.

As King McBeard stepped through the door, the coat of arms grabbed his hand and shook it. The king smiled a little bit. Downstairs, he saw some polka-dotted knights, and his smile grew. His smile stretched further as a knight ran by with a horse on his back.

"Hello, Sire," said the horse. "Fine day we're having."

"Neigh," snorted the knight.

Outside, the king saw his knight Sir Munch-a-Lot sitting on a meatball with a strand of spaghetti on his sword. In the moat, Sir Fing balanced on a raft of tomato chunks.

The royal chef sprinted from the castle. "No, no! Don't play with your food!" he shouted.

The storm cloud above King McBeard's head paled to pearly gray. When the knights saw their cheerful king, they gathered around him, laughing as they slipped, slid, and sprawled in the spaghetti sauce.

The king looked up at the cloud floating over his head. He pointed to it and started chortling. Then he guffawed. Finally, he let out a king-size belly laugh. *Poof!* The cloud vanished, leaving a rainbow in its place. As King McBeard wiped tears of laughter from his eyes, he asked, "Who could have caused these castle capers?"

Eli the Wizard appeared in a puff of purple smoke. "It was I, Sire," he said. "Thank you, my friend," said the king. "You have cured my Cloudophobia. But what if the cloud comes back? Can you help me remember how to laugh a royal belly laugh?"

"Why, Sire, that's easy," said the wizard. "It really takes no magic spell. The next time you feel grumpy, just use your imagination. Look at things in a new way, as you did just now." With that, Eli lifted the magic spell by saying the seven *s* words in reverse order.

The next day, the coat of arms was in its usual spot on the castle wall. The knights were once again dressed in gold. Everything was back to normal—well, almost everything.